Peachy and Keen

A SCHOOL TAIL

by Jason Tharp
and J. B. Rose

SCHOLASTIC INC.

Dedicated to my fellow dreamers:
Chase massive dreams,
practice when others would give up,
and be yourself, 'cause you're purrfect!

Be the weird YOU want
to see in the world!
—Jason

ISBN 978-1-338-11043-2

10 9 8 7 6 5 4 3 2 1   18 19 20 21 22

Printed in the U.S.A.   40
First printing 2018

Book design by Suzanne LaGasa

Contents

A Doggone Good Idea

"Keen? Helloooo, Earth to Keen!" Peachy the cat poked a tiny dog in a dinosaur costume.

"RAWRRRRRRR!" Keen jumped, startled. "Peachy, you scared me!"

"Were you daydreaming about cookies again?" Peachy asked.

"Umm," said Keen, "no?"

"Keen?"

"Well, okay, maybe," Keen admitted. "But you know how hungry I get after . . . *anything*. And today was the first day of school so I'm EXTRA hungry!"

Peachy laughed like it was perfectly normal to talk about chocolate-chip daydreams with a doggy in a dinosaur costume. Because when you were best friends with Keen—it was.

Peachy and Keen had been purrfect pals ever since they were little. Peachy was a cool, collected kitty, while Keen was, well, hungry. Keen was a friendly furball with a love of costumes and an even greater love of food. But while most of the cats and dogs at school didn't usually get along, somehow Peachy and Keen just worked.

"Well, you can daydream about chocolate-chip dog biscuits later." Peachy pulled Keen down the hall. "We have to go sign up for the school newspaper!"

"Aw, Peachy," Keen groaned. "Why do we have to join the *Happy Tails Times*? The students only read that paper when they want a good catnap."

"That's not true," Peachy said. "Besides, it's been my dream to write for the paper ever since . . . fur-ever! And this year, we're finally old enough to join."

Peachy pictured herself walking the halls with a notepad, wearing a fancy press badge to show everyone just how super important her writing was.

"My aunt was the star reporter when she was a student here," Peachy chattered on. "She covered all sorts of amazing stories. The Great Catscape, The Cow Who Cried Wolf, even Waterfowl Gate!"

"*ZZZZZZZ.*" Keen pretended to snore.

"Keen!" Peachy exclaimed.

"Sorry," Keen said. "But just thinking about it makes me dog-tired!"

"Well, then do it for me, as your best friend," Peachy pleaded.

The pair hurried down the crowded hallway. Classes had just finished, and the hall was full of students on their way to different after-school activities. Keen was smaller than most animals, so he had to keep dodging the bigger students to avoid getting smooshed.

"Watch it!" Keen exclaimed when two football-player rhinos almost stepped on his tail. "RAWRRR!" He let out his most impressive dinosaur growl.

"Did you hear something?" one rhino asked the other.

"Must have been my stomach." The second rhino patted his belly. "They were serving bug-ritos for lunch today. *URP.*"

Keen turned around. Gross!

Peachy was already at the far end of the hall. Keen sprinted to catch up. Peachy was chattering away like she hadn't even noticed he'd been missing. ". . . And I'm just so excited to write something really cool. You know, an article that will make a big difference in the school! I have tons of ideas. I've—" Peachy stopped very suddenly, causing Keen to run into her.

"Oof! Fuzzy furballs, Peachy." Keen rubbed his nose. "Why'd you stop?"

"I don't understand," Peachy said, confused. "This is the room where the newspaper meets. But it looks like no one is in here. Are we early?"

"Not exactly," a stern voice said behind them.

Peachy and Keen turned to see a giant elephant: Principal Trunx. He was famous at Happy Tails School for two things: his love of peanuts, and his love of the *rules*. Right now, Principal Trunx was staring down his trunk at them with his arms crossed.

"I'm afraid the *Happy Tails Times* is no more," he said.

Peachy was shocked. "What! Why?"

"We shut it down," Principal Trunx said, "due to a lack of interest."

"But . . . but that can't be true!" Peachy exclaimed. "It's been my dream to join the paper ever since I was a kitten. My aunt used to be the star reporter when she was a student here."

"Oh, I remember your aunt, Miss . . . Peachy, is it?" Principal Trunx narrowed his eyes. "Your aunt was *Purrfect* Priscilla. Always getting the big scoops. Leaving the rest of us to report on doggy doo-doo."

Peachy hadn't realized Principal Trunx and her aunt had been students at Happy Tails School together. But it didn't sound like they'd gotten along.

"Well, times have changed," Principal Trunx continued. "No one reads the paper anymore. And the *Happy Tails Handbook* specifically states that any school club with a lack of interest must be shut down."

"But how are students supposed to know what's happening around school?" Peachy insisted. "And how else am I supposed to become a star reporter?"

"I suggest you find a new hobby," Principal Trunx said brusquely. "One that doesn't follow in the paw prints of your aunt. Besides, the only things you hyper little furballs care about these days are your fancy gadgets with the texting and the Chimpstagram and whatever-you-call-it—"

Just then, a *BING* came from Keen's pocket. Keen reached for his PinePhone and giggled at something he saw on the screen. Peachy elbowed him to pay attention.

"You'll have to find something else to do," Principal Trunx finished. "Both of you!"

The principal stared at them awkwardly until Peachy and Keen slowly made their way down the hall.

"It's okay, Peachy," Keen said as soon as they were out of earshot. "Don't let Principal Cranky-Trunks get you down. At least now we can go for an after-school snack. I'm as hungry as a horse! And that's saying something. Oh, oh! Let's go to Pizza Mutt! No, no. McDonkey's? No! Nibbles 'n' Bits! What do you think is the Cookie of the Day? I hope it's Maple-Bacon Bash. No, Peanut Butter Bash. No, Choco-Chunk. No, no! Definitely Maple-Bacon—"

"I just can't believe there's no more paper," Peachy interrupted. "Just like that—something I've been looking forward to since fur-ever is . . . gone."

"Hey, I know it's rough," Keen said. "But cheer up! There are lots of other things we can do." Keen hopped around her, wagging his tail. "We could go play chase-the-tennis-ball-and-never-bring-it-back! Or practice our *RAWRS* at strangers passing the window! Or . . ."

"And what does Principal Trunx mean, 'no one reads the newspaper'?" She mimicked the principal's deep voice. "It's almost like he's *happy* the *Happy Tails Times* is shut down. There has to be a way to get students more excited about the school news!"

Suddenly, another *BING* came from Keen's PinePhone. "Woo-hoo!" he cheered, looking at the screen.

"There's going to be a new episode of *Hot Diggity Dog* tonight!"

As Peachy watched Keen on his phone, an idea started to come to her. "Wait . . ." she said. "Where are you reading that?"

"It's from a Hot Diggity Dog fan website," said Keen. "It sends updates to me when there's news about the show! It says in the episode tonight, Hot Diggity Dog captures the town bank robber with a lasso made out of bacon—"

Peachy's idea was growing. "News, you say?" she asked with a smile.

"Uh-huh . . ." Keen gave her a weird look. "Okay, so, are we going to Nibbles 'n' Bits or what? C'mon, c'mon, c'mon!"

But Peachy wasn't listening. She had just thought of a super-awesome, totally amazing, brilliant idea!

The Purrfect Pitch

"**Y**ou are a GENIUS!" Peachy shouted, pulling Keen into a hug.

"I know!" said Keen. "Wait, why?"

"Because!" said Peachy happily. "It's just like Principal Trunx said. Almost all students have PinePhones now.

What if we create a newspaper that they can read on their PinePhones? That will definitely get their attention!"

"Wow! I guess I am a bone-a-fide genius," said Keen, nodding.

"And," Peachy continued, "we could make it a digital magazine instead of a newspaper. We can write about all kinds of stuff!" The hamster wheels in Peachy's head were really turning now.

Fly's
ence
ner

Here's the rare look into the inner workings of the feline mind. Just look at those ideas cranking out.

"Rawr! That sounds dino-rific," Keen admitted, starting to get excited, too.

"With an idea this good, there's no way Principal

Trunx can say there will be a lack of interest!" Peachy clapped her paws. "But first we have to get organized." She pulled Keen toward their lockers so they could gather their things and get working.

"Okay, okay, but we're stopping at Nibbles 'n' Bits on the way home!" said Keen.

The next day, Peachy and Keen sat outside the principal's office. They had worked at Peachy's house all evening on ideas for the online magazine. They had even made a glittery poster to show off the design! It had been a little hard to keep Keen focused. Shiny things like glitter tended to distract him. But together, they had made an impressive presentation for Principal Trunx.

"You can go on in now, my dears," the secretary said.

Peachy and Keen gulped as they entered. Everything in Principal Trunx's office was so . . . *BIG*. Oversize chairs. Towering bookshelves. Even the books were the size of Peachy. She scanned the titles:

An Elephant Never Forgets: 101 Ways to Boost Your Memory

Going Nuts: Controlling Your Peanut Cravings in a Nut-Free World

Principal Trunx sat with his arms crossed behind a fancy wooden desk. "I only have a few minutes, so let's get on with it," he said.

Peachy sat up straight and cleared her throat. "Well, Principal Trunx, Keen and I think it's important that the students have somewhere to get information about their school—and somewhere to be creative! So we came up with a new idea to replace the old newspaper: *Purrfect9 Magazine!*"

She made a *ta-da* gesture as Keen held up their glittery poster.

Principal Trunx didn't look impressed, but Peachy kept going. "We want to start a digital magazine for the school. Students will get messages on their PinePhones when new articles are posted. And we'll write about all kinds of topics, like sports, fashion, food, school events, student interviews—anything you can think of!"

Suddenly, out of the corner of her eye, Peachy saw Keen inching toward something shiny on Principal Trunx's shelf. *Uh-oh*, she thought. Keen was getting distracted again. *I know he likes shiny things, but not now!*

"We can use the old newspaper room for meetings," Peachy added quickly, trying to wrap up before Principal Trunx spotted Keen.

The principal raised his eyebrows. "So other students are part of this idea of yours?"

"Um, well, right now it's just Keen and me," Peachy said. "But I'm sure we can get some more students to join."

"You'll have to!" Principal Trunx snapped. "According the *Happy Tails Handbook*, all student clubs must have at least six members."

"Easy-peasy, mousey-cheesy!" Keen shouted from behind Principal Trunx. He was playing with the elephant's shiny gold pocket watch. But it was as big as a dinner plate! Peachy gulped as Keen tried to lift it up.

"*And*," continued Principal Trunx, "you would be required to have a faculty member oversee this little magazine. Do you have one?"

"Um . . . we will!" Peachy assured him. "So . . . does that mean yes?"

Principal Trunx shook his head. "Your club doesn't meet any of the requirements."

Peachy sat up as tall as she could. Peachy knew rules. Peachy loved rules! And Peachy had rules on her side.

"The *Happy Tails Handbook* also says that any new clubs are allowed a trial week to get up and running," she said.

Principal Trunx frowned. Peachy was right. The handbook *did* say that.

"Fine." He snorted. "You can write the magazine as a *trial run*. But if you don't fill all the requirements by the end of the week, or I don't like what I see, the magazine will be over."

"Hooray!" Peachy and Keen cheered, sending glitter into the air and onto Principal Trunx.

"Argh! Get that sparkly nonsense out of here!" Principal Trunx blew glitter out of his trunk and waved them away.

Once they were out in the hallway, Keen jumped up and down. "I can't believe we did it! We got Principal Cranky-Trunks to agree! But boy, we've got a lot to do. Don't we?"

Peachy was too busy grinning from whisker to whisker to pay attention. They were going to start *Purrfect9*! Soon, she would be a star reporter, just like she'd always dreamed.

Okay, so first they'd need to find some students to join.

And a faculty advisor.

And some super-stellar story ideas.

But that couldn't be all that hard, right?

Wow, check out these awesome dream sparkles!

A Ruff Start

Peachy and Keen created flyers for *Purrfect9* so the other students would know about their club. Peachy couldn't wait for everyone to see it. Students would be lining up to join!

But as Peachy passed one of the flyers, she stopped. She furrowed her furry brow.

Someone had taped a different flyer over hers. And based on the theme, she had a sneaking suspicion who . . .

"Ahoy, matey! It's pretty good, right?" Keen said behind her.

Peachy turned and saw him wagging his tail. Today he wore a new pirate outfit, complete with a hook hand. "I hung up the flyers we made together," Keen said brightly. "But then I came up with a few new ones that are sure to convince students to join our crew! *Arrggh!*"

Peachy frowned. She was used to Keen's daydreams. But this was starting to interfere with their plan. With *her* dream. And she wasn't sure she liked it.

"Keen!" Peachy said, pulling down the flyer. "This flyer doesn't even make any sense. We're not giving away gold to join the magazine."

"We're not getting any gold, you say? *Arrgh*, then ye'll have to walk the plank!" Keen said. But when he saw Peachy's expression, he dropped the pirate accent. "Aw, come on, Peachy. You've gotta add some more excitement to get everyone's attention. I'm doing you a favor, you'll see."

"Sure you are," Peachy said, still a bit annoyed. "Well, are we still meeting during lunch to talk some other students into joining?"

"As sure as the wind blows, matey!"

It turned out convincing other students to join *Purrfect9* was trickier than Peachy expected. For one thing, a lot of students had already joined other after-school activities.

"Sorry, but I'm captain of the volleyball team," Gina the giraffe told them in the cafeteria as she munched on a leaf and twig salad.

Gina's friend Sheldon was also busy with sports. "I have track practice every day," the turtle said. "I have to train my shell off if I'm ever going to beat Rocky Rabbit at the hundred-meter dash!"

Keen looked confused. "But you're a turtle. Aren't you really slo—OW! *Arrgh*, what was that for, you scallywag?" Peachy had just stepped on Keen's foot.

"What my, uh, first mate here is saying," Peachy said to Sheldon, "is that I'm sure you'll beat Rocky in no time! Good luck!"

Next, Peachy and Keen went to the auditorium. But they didn't find any takers there, either.

"I just simply do not have the time," said Gisella the peacock. She ruffled her pretty feathers dramatically. "I have to work on my audition for *Beauty and the Geese*."

"Can't you rehearse *and* work on the magazine?" Peachy suggested hopefully.

"Oh my feathers!" Gisella huffed. "Some people don't understand that *true art* takes dedication and time!"

"So I guess that's a no." Peachy sighed.

By the end of the day, Peachy was feeling pretty down. "What are we going to do, Keen?" she asked. "I can't be the only one who thinks this is important."

But Keen wasn't listening. "Shiver me timbers!" he cried, playing with a paper airplane he'd folded out of a *Purrfect9* flyer. It had a little pirate pilot. "It's an air battle over Locker Sea!"

"I'm starting to think *you're* not interested, either," Peachy said.

That got Keen's attention. "I'm interested. I'm totally interested! Didn't I make those flyers with you? And roll in the glitter to show you how glittery it could be?

And didn't I go with you around school to round up a crew?" Keen wagged his tail like an eager puppy. "Didn't I? Didn't I?"

Peachy couldn't help giggling. That was one of the things she liked best about Keen. Even when she was down, he always had a way of making her smile.

But that didn't solve their problem.

"How are we supposed to get Principal Trunx to allow the magazine if we can't even get a staff?" she asked.

"What about her?" Keen pointed to a snooty-looking cat a few lockers down.

Peachy followed his gaze. "Ugh," she groaned. "I don't think *Rue* will want to join."

Rue was a high-fashion kitty with an even higher-minded attitude. Her dad was the CEO of Calico Computers—the city's leading tech company. That made her think she was better than everyone else.

"What have we got to lose?" Keen asked. "As sure as the sea, a potential reporter she be!"

Peachy sighed and walked over to Rue. "Hi, Rue," she said. "We're starting an online magazine, and I thought—"

Peachy paused under Rue's snooty stare.

"You thought *what*?" Rue asked huffily.

"We thought you might want to join!" Keen said.

Rue looked Keen up and down in his pirate costume.

"*Why* are you dressed like that?"

"I'm a pirate!" Keen grinned. He tossed his pirate airplane into the air . . . and *BOINK*—it hit Rue right in the face!

She scowled and unfolded the paper. "An online magazine?" She read the flyer. "*Whose* idea was that?"

"Yes, and it was my idea." Peachy said defensively. She didn't like the way Rue made everything sound beneath her. In fact, she wasn't sure she wanted Rue to join at all.

"Forget we mentioned it," Peachy said, taking the flyer. "I'm sure you have *better* things to do."

Before Rue could make another snide comment, Peachy walked away. But her shoulders slumped.

No one in the entire school seemed to be excited about the magazine. It looked like *Purrfect9* would be over before it even started.

A Motley Zoo

The next afternoon, the last bell of the day rang out in the hallways. That sound meant the official start of all after-school activities. Peachy began to walk toward the old newspaper room, which was soon to be the headquarters for *Purrfect9 Magazine*—that is, if there was a *Purrfect9*.

Peachy was sure that no one but Keen would show up to the first meeting. *And even Keen might be late, depending on what the Cookie of the Day at Nibbles 'n' Bits is . . .* she thought.

But as Peachy rounded the corner, she gasped. A small group of students was gathered in front of the meeting room! There was Connie the octopus, Nanner the monkey, and Gertie, the one and only unicorn at Happy Tails School. Gertie was one of the most popular students in class. Peachy couldn't believe *she* wanted to join!

"Are you guys all here for *Purrfect9?*" Peachy asked in disbelief.

"They sure are!" Keen came skidding around the corner dressed in a disco outfit. "I convinced them all to join!"

"You did?" Peachy's voice caught in her throat. "Keen, that's amazing! Thank you!" This had to be the best thing Keen had ever done for her. He had really pulled through!

Peachy turned to her new staff. "Okay, everyone, let's go in!"

"Um, I'm not sure we can." Gertie nodded toward the closed classroom door. "Someone is already in there."

Peachy heard faint music coming from inside the classroom. She peeked through the door window. Inside was a llama named Rocco, the school janitor—but he wasn't cleaning.

"EVERYBODY PRANCE NOW!" Rocco danced across the floor, bopping his head and strutting to the music.

Peachy opened the door, but Rocco had the music turned up so loud he didn't hear her. "Um, excuse me!" Peachy called.

Rocco finally looked over and saw the group of students staring at him. He gave them a big grin. "Hey there, my cool cats and bodacious beasts! Are you here to join the dance party?"

Peachy said, "Actually, we're supposed to be having a meeting in here," at the same time that Keen shouted, "Yeah!"

"Cool, cool, sorry about that," Rocco apologized. He turned down the music. "I'm used to this room being empty. I'll just take my fiesta somewhere else!" The llama gave them a peace sign before boogying out of the room.

"That was . . . different," said Nanner.

"Okay, everyone!" Peachy announced as she started pushing the tables and chairs back into place. "I'm Peachy, and I'm so happy you all decided to join *Purrfect9*. Let's take a seat and introduce ourselves. You can each share why you want to join the magazine!"

She looked at the group expectantly, but no one wanted to go first. For a moment, there was awkward silence.

Crickets.

Oh, wait, Peachy realized. *Those are just the crickets in the Critter Club meeting next door.*

Still, it was really quiet. No one wanted to go first. Peachy looked at Connie. "How about you?" she asked.

Connie smiled. "Okay. Hi, everyone! I'm Connie!" She waved her many tentacles in greeting, one of which was bandaged. "I used to play for the hockey team, but I got hurt at practice: Some rookie walrus got me with his teeth instead of the puck."

Everyone winced in sympathy.

"Coach said I'd be out the whole season," Connie continued. "My spirits totally tanked, but then Keen told me all about how I could have VIP box seats to every sporting event in town if I joined the magazine!"

MAN, YOU'RE SPECIAL!

Peachy raised an eyebrow. "VIP box seats?" she asked. "We can get you a press pass to student sporting events. But I don't know about every event in town."

Connie looked a little disappointed. "Oh. Okay. Well, I guess writing about sports is the next best thing to playing them, anyway."

Peachy looked to the monkey sitting next to Connie. "How about you?"

"I'm Nanner." The monkey straightened his polka-dot bow tie. "I'm ready to see some celebrities! When Keen told me about all the red-carpet perks of writing for the magazine, I almost went bananas! Do you think I can meet Meryl Sheep?"

Peachy was starting to get a bad feeling. "Probably not," she said slowly. She looked over to Keen, who was distracted by a *Hot Diggity Dog* game on his PinePhone.

"Keen, why did you tell everyone that joining the magazine would have special perks?"

"It doesn't?" He looked up from his phone, surprised.

"Noooo," Peachy said. "What made you think that?"

"Huh," said Keen. "I guess I wrote fun stuff like that on so many of the flyers I made, I thought it was real!"

Peachy looked around. "Is that the reason all of you decided to join? Because you thought there would be fancy perks?"

"Not me," Gertie spoke up. Her voice chimed like crystal, and sparkles floated from her cotton-candy-pink mane as she shook her head. "I wanted to join *Purrfect9* because it sounds fun! And I thought I could write articles that give students advice about everyday things. You know, like, tips to get ready for hibernation season. Or how to tell your tiger parents that you want to become an herbivore."

Peachy beamed. At least someone in the group actually seemed excited about the magazine! "That's a great idea, Gertie!"

Just then, the door opened. And in walked . . . Rue!

"We're having a meeting in here," Peachy said.

Rue huffed. "I *know* that. I've come to join."

Everyone's jaws dropped. A little "GAME OVER" sound effect came from Keen's *Hot Diggity Dog* game.

"You do?" Peachy asked.

Rue strutted over. Her silver bangle bracelets jingled as she walked. "Don't act so surprised." She pulled up a chair to join the group. "I like to write. And you *said* there would be a fashion section. If you'd stayed to listen yesterday, I would have told you that I think this school is in need of fashion advice." Rue eyed Keen's shark costume. "Desperately."

"Okay . . ." Peachy said hesitantly. Then, she smiled. "Well, okay! I guess that makes six of us. And according to the *Happy Tails Handbook*, that's just the number of students we need."

Despite the rocky start, Peachy's hopes were growing. *Purrfect9 Magazine* had a full staff and was one step closer to becoming an official school club.

And she was one step closer to her dream!

Selfies and Suspicious Smells

"Ugh, that smell in our meeting room is getting worse every day!" Nanner complained. "It's worse than a rhino's butt! Didn't you say Rocco was going to come see what it was?"

"He was supposed to," Peachy said. "But I guess he must be really busy."

It had been almost a week since the first meeting of *Purrfect9*. For the most part, things were going really well. Everyone had come up with cool ideas for their magazine sections.

Peachy was covering school news and interviews. And Nanner was writing entertainment reviews called "Funky Monkey Movie and Musical Madness."

Gertie had started a self-help column titled "Gracious Gertie." So far she'd written advice for a dog who kept accidentally eating his own homework and a porcupine who just wanted a hug.

Rue had turned out to be the biggest surprise of all. Because her dad was a tech guru, she had a knack for creating digital slideshows where students could swipe through pictures of style dos and don'ts. Her articles looked super professional.

"These are awesome!" Peachy said, swiping through a slick slideshow of the best bangles for Bengal cats. Maybe she had misjudged Rue. In fact, Peachy was *this* close to liking her.

Rue snorted. "Of *course* they're awesome." She looked Peachy up and down. "Am I *really* the only one at this school with *any* style sense?"

Peachy sighed. "So close," she said under her breath.

But even though everyone had been working hard, there were still a couple of problems.

First, Peachy was having difficulty finding a faculty member to be their advisor. All the teachers seemed to be busy.

And then there was the *smell*. Ever since their second meeting, a horrible stench had been wafting from the ceiling vent. Rocco the janitor was supposed to come fix it. But he hadn't shown up—and it was difficult to type with one paw and cover your nose with the other.

"It's not so bad if you sit over here," Gertie called

from the far end of the classroom. She had stuffed cotton-candy balls up her nostrils.

"No, it's pretty bad," insisted Nanner. "Like, I have a crazy uncle who has a weird habit of collecting rotten banana peels. And he keeps them in his basement. *This* is worse."

Just then, Connie and Keen came barging in. Connie had gone to write about the school football game: The Happy Tails Tigers versus the Pawcademy Pirates. Keen had gone with her to take photos. But Connie had an annoyed look on her face.

"Rough game?" Peachy asked.

"I wouldn't call it a game. More like a total dogfight!" Connie shouted.

"Our friend Connie is just a little competitive," Keen stage-whispered to the rest of the group.

"The ref was totally blind!" Connie argued. "That bat missed *everything*!"

"Can you still write about the game?" Peachy asked.

"Oh, you bet I can write about it!" Connie sat down and began typing at her computer, her tentacles waving wildly. "Gonna give that bat a piece of my mind . . ."

Peachy turned to Keen. "How did the photos come out?" she asked eagerly.

"Super fantastic!" Keen beamed. Ever since the game, he'd been dressed as the Happy Tails Tigers' football mascot: Saber the Siberian. "Take a look at all the great shots I got!"

Peachy scanned through the photos. Keen had captured tons of game action shots. But covering each picture was a familiar face.

"Keen . . . why are you in all of these photos?" Peachy asked.

"I took mascot selfies!" Keen exclaimed. "To show the game AND school spirit!"

Peachy shook her head. "But we can't see the game with your tiger head covering all the players. Don't you have any pictures without you in them? Any at all?"

Before he could answer, Rocco finally arrived, holding a ladder and a toolbox. "I hear there's a gnarly smell putting your club in a skunk funk!" he said cheerfully. "Never fear, Rocco is here. Where is it coming fro—oh, never mind." Rocco wrinkled his nose as he walked right beneath the vent. "Whew! That smells worse than a rhino's butt."

"That's what I said!" cried Nanner.

Rocco set his ladder against the wall and pulled out a screwdriver to open the vent. The *Purrfect9* staff watched in suspense, waiting to see what was inside.

Suddenly, Rocco gasped. "No way, man! My sandwich! I knew I put this bad boy somewhere!" He pulled out a paper wrapper that held something that may have once been a sandwich, but now looked like something Nanner's uncle stored in his basement.

Gertie's face turned green. So did her mane.

"What's all this?" came the voice of Principal Trunx. He was standing in the doorway, frowning. "Doesn't look like much work is getting done here!"

Peachy jumped up. "Rocco was just helping us with a slight problem."

"But problem solved!" Rocco said as he climbed down the ladder. "Smell problem solved *and* dinner problem solved." He picked up his ladder and bopped out of the room.

"He's not really going to *eat* that, is he?" Connie whispered to Gertie behind a tentacle.

Gertie turned a shade greener.

"Well, I'd say bad smells are the *least* of your problems, Miss Peachy." Principal Trunx crossed his arms. "This club still has no adult supervisor. And you know the rules. You can't have a club without an advisor."

Peachy gulped. "I've been trying! I just need a couple more days to find someone."

"You don't have a couple days," said Principal Trunx. "Your one-week trial period ends tomorrow. If you don't have an advisor by then, this magazine is over."

A Sketchy Surprise

Principal Trunx left the room in a huff—and left Peachy feeling more anxious than ever.

"What are we going to do?" She buried her face in her paws. "I've asked every single teacher in the school. No one will agree to be our advisor."

"Did you try Mr. Mulbearry, the forest conservation teacher?" Gertie asked.

Peachy looked up. "I thought he was on hibernation vacation?"

Gertie shook her head. Shimmery sparkles floated down to the floor. "I saw him sniffing around the cafeteria this morning. I guess he's getting a late start."

Peachy's eyes lit up. "If he's going on vacation, he can't have other clubs to oversee. But maybe he'd agree to be our advisor remotely! We are a digital magazine, after all."

She logged off her computer and grabbed her bag. "It's worth a shot. Meanwhile, everyone go ahead and post your finished articles—our magazine goes live tomorrow morning. Rue, maybe you can help Keen fix some of his photos to look less selfie and more game-y."

Rue eyed Keen's pictures. "Doubtful," she said.

"Just do your best," Peachy called, hurrying out of the room. "*Purrfect9* just has to be perfect. It has to be!"

Once Peachy was gone, Nanner shook his head. "She sure takes this stuff seriously, doesn't she?"

"That's just how Peachy is," said Keen. "She likes everything to be, well, peachy."

"How come you two are friends?" Rue asked, starting to edit Keen's mascot selfies.

"Yeah, you two don't really seem like you go together," Connie added.

Keen shrugged and started doodling in his notebook. "Peachy's been my best friend since we were just a kitten and a pup, fur-ever and ever! She thinks everything I do is funny. We're like peanut butter and jelly. Nothing could come between us."

"Speaking of sandwiches, I'm so glad that smell is gone." Gertie finally took the cotton-candy balls out of her nose.

"Seriously," said Nanner. "How could he have forgotten his sandwich for so long?" He had just finished uploading his movie reviews to *Purrfect9*.

"I think the real question," asked Rue, "is *why* would he put a sandwich in the vent in the first place?"

"Maybe he accidentally threw it up there doing one of his boogie-woogie dance moves." Keen chuckled. He began drawing a sketch of Rocco doing the tango with his mop. He added a giant sandwich flying out of his hands to complete the illustration.

ROCCO'S BEST PLACES TO HIDE A SANDWICH

1. The refrigerator — TOO Obvious!

2. In a shoe — Too Stinky

3. In a ceiling vent → PERFECT!

4. In a book — NO, BUT FUNNY!

BOOK WICH

"Hey, that's pretty good," Nanner said, looking over Keen's shoulder. "You guys, come check this out!"

"This is hilarious, Keen!" Connie said.

"You think so?" Keen wagged his tail.

"Yeah!" exclaimed Nanner. "It looks just like Rocco! You should totally upload this to the magazine."

Keen stopped wagging his tail. "I don't know," he said slowly. "I should ask Peachy first."

"But I thought you said she thinks everything you do is funny." Connie pointed out.

"Yeah," Rue added. "Nothing could *ever* come between you two."

Keen still looked uncertain. "I know. But this magazine is really important to Peachy."

"And your cartoon will make it better!" exclaimed Gertie. "We all think it's funny, don't we?"

Everyone nodded.

"It could be like bonus surprise content," Gertie said. "Peachy will love it!"

Impressing his classmates made Keen feel good. "Okay, yeah! It'll be a surprise! I'll post it to the website now." Keen scanned his cartoon into the computer. Once it was loaded onto the *Purrfect9* database, he added a title: Make Way for Ra-Ra-Rocco and the Incredibly Stinky Sandwich!

PURRFECT9 ♥ EXCLUSIVE By: Keen

Make Way for Ra-Ra-Rocco and the Incredibly Stinky Sandwich!

"All right!" Nanner cheered. "Just wait—tomorrow everyone in the whole school will see that."

"Everyone in the whole school?" Keen repeated. He hadn't thought of it that way. But then he looked back at

the cartoon and smiled. The others were right—
everyone was sure to love it.

Especially Peachy. Right?

Llama Drama

The next morning, Peachy was back to square one. Even Mr. Mulbearry had turned her down.

"Sorry, Peachy." He'd let out a great big yawn. "But I'm going off the grid for my vacation this year. No Internet access. Just me, nature, and *ZZZZZZZZZZ*." He'd fallen asleep.

Her only hope now was that Principal Trunx would be so impressed by *Purrfect9* that he'd give her extra time to find a faculty advisor.

Speaking of which . . . she thought excitedly. She pulled out her PinePhone. She'd been so busy tracking down the teacher that she hadn't made it back to the classroom before it closed to review the final magazine. But she trusted her team. And she couldn't wait to see her dream go live!

Sure enough, at 8:30 a.m. on the dot, Peachy's PinePhone buzzed.

Peachy squealed with excitement. The message had worked! She looked around her and saw other students also receiving the message on their PinePhones. Peachy clicked the link and scrolled through the headlines:

"Happy Tails School to Host
Parrot-Teacher Conference"
by Peachy

"Gracious Gertie Advises Porcupine
in Prickly Situation"
by Gertie

"Behind the Scenes of
Beauty and the Geese"
by Nanner

"*Style*: Get Some"
by Rue

"Pawcademy Pirates Beat Happy Tails Tigers
(Because Ref Needs Glasses)"
by Connie

"Make Way for Ra-Ra-Rocco and
the Incredibly Stinky Sandwich!"
A cartoon by Keen

Wait—what was that?

Peachy clicked on the last link. Up popped a silly cartoon of Rocco dancing.

Peachy gasped. Keen had never asked her if he could publish this. She'd never even *seen* it! How could he do this without telling her?

Peachy sprinted toward Keen's locker.

"Howdy-ho, Peachy!" Keen said with a grin. He was dressed as a cowboy. "Today's the big day! Did you see the magazine? Did you? Did you?"

"Keen, what is *this*?" Peachy held up the cartoon.

"Pretty clever, right?" Keen asked excitedly. "Is it a rootin' tootin' riot or what?"

Peachy was practically shaking. "How could you do this to me?" she asked.

"Whoa, whoa, settle down there, partner." Keen frowned. "You sound mad."

"Of course I'm mad!" Peachy exclaimed. "You published this cartoon without asking me! I'm the Editor in Chief. I'm supposed to know what's in the magazine!"

"But Gertie and Nanner and all of them thought it was really funny," Keen said. "I thought you'd love it."

There she blows!

"Well, I *don't*," Peachy yelled. "We can't publish a cartoon that makes fun of someone like that."

"I wasn't making fun of anyone." Keen's eyes got wide. "I was just being silly."

"Exactly! You never take anything seriously!" Peachy raised her voice so loud that *everyone* stopped to look at them. "You're always goofing around. And now you've ruined my magazine!"

"Hey!" Keen was growing angry now, too. "*Purrfect9* is just as much mine as it is yours. We started it together."

"You've done nothing but slow it down from the beginning," Peachy snapped. "First you came up with those silly flyers talking about gold giveaways. Meanwhile, you folded *my* flyers into paper airplanes."

"Rue would never have even known about *Purrfect9* if I hadn't hit her with my airplane," Keen said.

"Then you made everyone think they'd get crazy VIP perks if they joined," Peachy said.

"But half the team signed up because of that!" Keen insisted.

"Then you took all those selfies in that *costume* on the football field," Peachy added.

Ouch. That hurt.

"It's called *school pride*," Keen said through gritted teeth.

"And now this!" Peachy waved the cartoon. "Principal Trunx will shut us down for sure!"

"Look, I know this is serious business for you," Keen said. "But some of us are just trying to have fun. I'm only part of this dumb magazine because YOU made me join. So if you don't like my ideas, then I QUIT!"

With that, Keen growled at her and ran away.

Peachy was left standing alone, trying very hard not to cry.

What had just happened?

Purrfect9 was over, and it looked like her friendship with Keen could be over, too.

Best Friends Fur-ever

It was lunch period, and Peachy was miserable. She'd avoided Keen and the other *Purrfect9* staff members all morning. A few classmates had congrat-ulated her on the magazine, and yesterday that would have made her ecstatic. But now all she could think about was how this would be their first and last issue.

They still didn't have an advisor. And without Keen, they didn't have enough members. Even if Principal Trunx didn't call them out on Keen's cartoon, there was no way he would let *Purrfect9* continue.

And worst of all, Keen hated her. She'd lost her biggest dream and her best friend all in one morning.

Peachy shuffled to her locker. That was when she a note taped to the front.

Peachy,
Please meet me in room 315 at lunch. Very important!
—Rocco

This is what is known in the animal kingdom as dead meat!

Mr. Fly's Science Corner

Peachy felt a lump in her throat. Oh no. Rocco must be furious.

She took a deep breath and headed to room 315. She opened the door and sure enough, Rocco was waiting for her. But to her surprise, next to Rocco was—

"Keen!" she cried. "What are you doing here?"

"Rocco told me to meet him here," Keen said.

Peachy looked from Rocco to Keen and back again. "Look, Rocco," she started, "I'm really sorry about the cartoon. I mean, I didn't even *know* about it." She shot Keen a look. "But I'm the Editor in Chief of *Purrfect9*, and I should have made sure it never got published."

"Never got published?" Rocco asked. "No way, my cool cat! That cartoon was totally far out!"

"It . . . was?" Peachy asked.

"Told you he'd like it," Keen said a bit bitterly.

"If you're not mad, then why did you tell us to meet you here?"

"Because I heard you two bodacious buddies shouting

this morning," Rocco said. "And I wondered what could have come between such furry friends."

"Well," Peachy started, "Keen didn't show me his cartoon before publishing it."

"I shouldn't have to get your permission for everything," Keen snapped.

Peachy's cheeks flushed. "Well, you shouldn't just go doing whatever you want."

"Whoa, whoa, whoa!" Rocco whistled with his toes.

"The energy in this room is *not* groovy. Now, I've only known you two since"—Rocco looked at his watch—"Wednesday. But I've seen you working on the magazine every day this week. You two cool critters are always in sync. You know, like peanut butter and jelly. Like burgers and fries. Like—"

"Peachy and Keen," Peachy said softly.

"Right on!" said Rocco. "So you're telling me that a silly doodle got in the way of your friendship?"

Peachy and Keen were quiet for a moment.

"I only wanted to make the magazine better," Keen said finally. "I wasn't trying to mess things up."

"You should always check with your editor before

you publish something." Rocco nodded seriously. "My lawyer once told me that."

Peachy and Keen gave Rocco a funny look.

"And I wasn't trying to take away your fun," said Peachy. "It's just, this magazine is super important to me," she continued. "My aunt used to tell me stories of how she was a star reporter here and how it was the beginning of her career. And it didn't seem like you were taking it seriously at all."

"I *am* taking it seriously!" Keen insisted. "Just my kind of serious, Peachy. And I'm seriously sorry."

"So . . ." Peachy said hesitantly. "Are we friends again?"

Keen tipped his cowboy hat. "You know it, partner!"

Peachy ran over and grabbed him in a big bear hug.

"Now, that's what I'm talking about!" Rocco gave them two thumbs-up. "The mega magazine duo is back in business."

"Thanks, Rocco," said Peachy. "But I think *Purrfect9* is on the last of its nine lives. We still don't have an adult advisor. Principal Trunx is going to shut us down."

"Aw, man, not cool." Rocco shook his head. "Hey, maybe I can help you find one. I'm an adult. I bet I could track another one down."

"It has to be a Happy Tails School staff member," Keen said.

"And I asked everyone," Peachy added. "I tried the teachers' lounge and the auditorium. I even tried the faculty meeting."

"Yeah, those meetings are a total bore," Rocco said.

Peachy looked at him. "You mean, you attend the faculty meetings?"

"Yeah, man," said Rocco. "Every week for ten years. The *Happy Tails Handbook* requires it."

Happy ☆ Tails ☆ Handbook

Rocco

RULES
1. Stay groovy
2. Clean stuff
3. Attend weekly faculty meeting

"Is that so?" Peachy asked. The hamster wheels in her head were turning again.

This kitty is creating ideas at the speed of light.

Mr. Fly's Science Corner

"Uh, Peachy?" Rocco waved a hand in front of her face. "What's wrong with her?" he asked Keen.

"Eh, this happens sometimes," Keen said, shrugging. "She's onto something. Just go with it."

Peachy was smiling, alert again. "Rocco, how would you like to advise one of the hippest new clubs at Happy Tails School?"

Rocco looked over his left shoulder. Then over his right. "Who, me?" he asked. He smiled a big toothy Rocco smile. "Far out!"

Later that day, the entire *Purrfect9* staff was gathered in room 315. They were all celebrating the success of their first issue. Nanner had brought everyone's favorite drinks: milk for Peachy, Kitty-Min Water for Rue, salt water for Connie, grapefruit soda for Gertie, rootin' tootin' root beer for Keen, and a banana smoothie for himself.

That was when Principal Trunx stomped in.

"Howdy, partner!" Keen raised his canteen. "You're just in time to join the party!"

Principal Trunx cleared his throat. "Actually, I'm here to break up the party. You've failed to find a faculty advisor, and according to the *Happy Tails Handbook*, I must officially shut down—"

"Hey, hey, hey, the fiesta has officially arrived!" Rocco bounced in holding a big bowl of hummus and cheetah-chips.

Principal Trunx looked annoyed. "I was just informing the students that this club will be shut down due to lack of adult supervision."

"But these bodacious beasts *do* have adult supervision." Rocco grinned. "Me!"

"I—you—what?!" Principal Trunx sputtered in surprise.

"Rocco is an official faculty member according to the *Happy Tails Handbook*," Peachy said, plopping down a copy of the handbook onto the desk in front of Principal Trunx. "So he qualifies as a club advisor." The rules were on her side again!

Principal Trunx narrowed his eyes. "That may be. But there's still the matter of the cartoon. We can't have students just writing about members of the Happy Tails School staff."

Peachy and Keen gulped.

Rocco chimed in. "Naw, principal dude. I gave them permission to write about me. No harm, no fowl!"

Principal Trunx eyed Rocco suspiciously.

Rocco cleared his throat. "Of course, I'll make sure they don't do it again, sir. I'll keep a close eye on them. As their adult supervisor." He winked at Peachy and Keen.

"So you see," Peachy said to Principal Trunx with a smile, "there's really no reason to shut down *Purrfect9*. We're following all the rules."

After a long pause, Principal Trunx sighed. "It would seem you are. But don't think this means I'm not watching you very closely." He turned and stomped out the door.

"Yee-haw! We're back in business!" cheered Keen.

The friends all whooped and high-fived.

"This is awesome!" said Connie. "I can't wait to give that bat another piece of my mind."

"It's better than awesome," said Nanner. "It's bananas!"

"I suppose it's *fine*," Rue said with a small smile.

"It's stellar!" Gertie's voice chimed.

"It's totally radical," said Rocco.

Peachy looked gratefully at her classmates. "Seems like this is the start of something really good."

"Mmmm." Keen said. "Did somebody say food?"

A few weeks later . . .
HAVE
SPIRIT
IS
DO YOU HAVE TH
May the best unicorn win!

To continued . . .